THE NOT-YETI

The story and all the pictures in
The Not-Yeti are original and have been
specially commissioned for Tesco.

Published for
Tesco Stores Limited
by Brilliant Books Ltd
84–86 Regent Street
London W1R 6DD

First published 1998

Text and Illustrations © 1998 Brilliant Books Ltd
Printed by Cambus Litho Ltd, Scotland
Reproduction by Graphic Ideas Studios, England

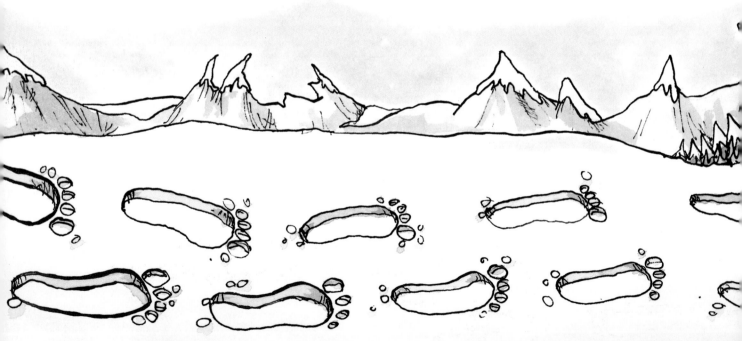

fun to learn

collection

THE NOT-YETI

Written by **Glenn Dakin**

Illustrated by **Mike Gibbie**

Think of the highest, coldest, snowiest, farest away place in the world. Now, go a little bit further, and you will be in the land of the Not-Yeti.

On this day, like every other day, the Not-Yeti was just about to head out of his cave. He'd decided to scare a few climbers just before they put their flag on top of Mount Everest. But...what if they had a camera and took a picture of him? He didn't like the idea of that!

"Oo-er! I'll scare some climbers one day – but not yet. Not yet... tomorrow perhaps..."

The only trouble was, when tomorrow came he always put his plans off, again! In fact, he put off EVERYTHING. That was why he was known as the Not-Yeti. He had not made an appearance for so long that most people didn't believe he was real.

However, in a valley far below, there was great excitement. The famous explorer, Sir Tinley Knott had arrived – to prove that the yeti really did exist.

"You must be very excited, Sir Tinley!" said a TV reporter.

"Certainly not!" said Sir Tinley Knott. "Excitement doesn't come into it. It's purely a matter of routine. Look, it's here in my schedule." He showed them a piece of paper. "Tomorrow: get up, have breakfast, climb Everest, have lunch, discover yeti, go home, bed. No room for excitement at all. Goodbye."

And off he strode, without saying another word.

Meanwhile, the Not-Yeti was sitting at home,
almost-but-not-quite writing a letter
to his friend, the Loch Ness Monster.
He decided to climb up to his Listening Place among
the high rocks, where the whispering wind brought all the news
of the mountains to his sensitive yeti ears. On the wind he heard
all about Sir Tinley Knott.

"How wonderful!" he thought. "A chance to meet a famous
explorer. I shall go and let him discover me right away!"

He zoomed off down the mountain on a tea tray that
had been left behind by some climbers.

But half way down, he stopped. "Suppose Sir Tinley offers me tea and biscuits? Suppose he doesn't like me? Oo-er! Suppose it turns out I don't really exist after all!" He sat by the Great Icicle and thought. "I'll let someone find me one day. But not yet! Not yet!" not-yetted the Not-Yeti.

That evening, there was a beautiful sunset, but Sir Tinley was too busy making camp half way up the mountain to notice.

"It will be incredible if there is a yeti!" said one of his team.
Sir Tinley snapped, "It will all be routine. Find yeti. Catch yeti.
Ask him if he exists. Write it down. Home, cocoa, bed. No excitement,
nothing unusual or incredible!"

The next day, the Not-Yeti was at home, trying not to think about being discovered. He nearly began work on his snowball-firing machine, almost perfected his recipe for snow-flavoured ice cream, and didn't quite get round to writing a pop song on his icicle xylophone.

Finally, curiosity overcame him. He decided to go
and see what a famous explorer looked like.

Sir Tinley was climbing higher and higher looking for the Not-Yeti, not realising the Not-Yeti was looking for him! A blizzard started to rage. In the driving snow, Sir Tinley lost his team, but still he pressed on.

When the snow began to stop, Sir Tinley looked around. He had wandered out on to an ice ledge jutting right out above a sheer drop. His team caught sight of him just as the ice shelf started to crack! At any moment, he would plunge to his doom!

Across a chasm, the Not-Yeti was watching from behind a rock. Only he could save Sir Tinley. But if he did, he might be seen! Everyone would know he existed! And he wouldn't be able to put things off 'til tomorrow any more!

Poor Sir Tinley saw the ice under him slowly shattering.

"Not yet! Not yet!" the Not-Yeti told himself hurriedly. "Maybe I'll start saving people tomorrow!"

KER-AAACK!

The ice broke. Suddenly, the Not-Yeti sprang into action. With all his abominable strength he leapt across the chasm. And just as Sir Tinley was about to fall, a blur of white fur appeared from nowhere and caught him! They crash-landed on the mountain slope, and rolled down it, forming a giant snowball.

At the bottom, the snowball hit a rock and the Not-Yeti and Sir Tinley Knott emerged — safe, but dizzy! They stared at each other for what seemed like ages.

"Goodness me!" said Sir Tinley. "Rescued by a mythical monster! For once in my life I can't think of anything to say!"

The Not-Yeti thought hard.

"Tea and biscuits?" he suggested.

The Not-Yeti led Sir Tinley up to his cave. There was so much he wanted to do, but had always put off. And Sir Tinley was so good at getting things done, but he'd never really enjoyed doing them.

Soon, they were planning all sorts of adventures together. "First, let's visit your friend the Loch Ness Monster!" said Sir Tinley. "I'll draw up a schedule. We'll start straight away!"

"Oh dear, I'd rather not," said the Not-Yeti. "Let's start tomorrow! Look at that lovely sunset!"